Brody's
Story

DATE DUE			

The Wings of Klaio

Book One

Brody's Story

Laura J. Boggess

OakTara

WATERFORD, VIRGINIA

Brody's Story

Published in the U.S. by:
OakTara Publishers
P.O. Box 8
Waterford, VA 20197

Visit OakTara at
www.oaktara.com

Cover design by David LaPlaca/debest design co.
Cover image, girl © iStockphoto.com/Michael Kemter
Cover image, dove © iStockphoto.com/Christopher Ewing

Author photo © 2007 Teddy and Jeffrey Boggess

Scripture verses are taken from the *Holy Bible*, New International Version®. NIV®. Copyright © 1973, 1978, 1984 by International Bible Society. Used by permission of Zondervan. All rights reserved.

ISBN: 978-1-60290-058-5

*To anyone
who has ever felt alone
in this world.
You are never alone, Beloved.
God is with you.
He is always, always with you.*

Acknowledgments

Thank you, my dear husband, for your endless support and encouragement.

To my beautiful friends, Vea and Melissa: thank you for believing in me.

And to my two gorgeous boys, Teddy and Jeffy; you never cease to inspire me!

But most of all, I thank my Heavenly Father, for being with me through it all.

One

She had been since the beginning of time. She was there in the Garden, and she witnessed the first lie. She witnessed the first sin. As she spread her wings to fly to the Lord, the eyes of the serpent caught her own and her heart was turned to stone. She felt her wings, once supple and light, turn to lead around her. As she fell to the ground the world began to spin, never to be the same again.

Eve, seeking her favored one, later found her there and, distraught, gathered the bird up in her hands. For she, the first woman, had loved the little bird since the first beat of her tiny winged heart. As Eve's tears bathed the bird's leaden body, they stained her stony feathers a rainbow of colors, the shades of human sorrow. And Eve called her Klaio, for her new appearance reflected the grief in all of heaven and earth.

Eve protected her all of the days that she lived on Earth. And from that point on, the bird was passed down from generation to generation, from life to life, to those who needed her. Over the centuries Klaio had seen much pain through her two jeweled eyes. Redemption did not come to all, for not all chose to open their hearts, but she helped deliver many. All hands that held her, as Eve had, had the opportunity to feel her healing power, the power of the first repentance. And as for Klaio? It was only inside the hearts of others that she was able to fly again, to spread her wings and soar. The Lord's authority was in her...His passionate love for all creation, locked inside her stony heart.

And so it was through time and God's will that Klaio came to be sitting on the bureau of twelve-year-old Brody Whitaker. After all, every one of us is a descendant of Eve. Brody knew nothing of the bird's esteemed past. She knew only that when she looked at the small vibrant cut of stone, peace filled her up inside.

As she stared into Klaio's crystal eyes now, a cloud washed over the pale blue of her own, and Brody sighed heavily. She gently picked the bird up and held it to her heart. The Lord's voice exploded in the bird's ears: *Fly! Fly, Klaio! Into the heart!*

As Brody's tender hands fluttered around the bird's breast, the creature flew. She flew unbeknownst into that child's heart and looked out through her eyes. She saw what Brody saw. She felt what Brody felt. And her heart was heavy with sorrow.

Brody gingerly placed the bird in the box before her. She would take this trinket with her wherever she went. It was one of the few things she had left of Grandma Pat. It reminded her of happier times.

They were moving tomorrow. They were moving because her mother no longer loved her father. And so they were going away from him. Brody would not miss her dad too much. Or so she thought. He was never here anyway. He was always working an odd shift at the factory, or sleeping or...well, just not himself.

No, it wasn't her father that she would miss. It was all that she knew. She looked out her window at the trees gently swaying in the breeze. They would have to leave this place. The secret spots she and her brothers and sister had discovered in the surrounding wood would be left behind. Her mother had found an apartment in town that was close to where she would be attending secretarial school. When she had shown it to the children, Brody was conscious of fear gnawing inside her. The starkness of the concrete that led up to the front door settled heavily in her heart.

She looked around. She would have to leave her room. Her sanctuary. She looked longingly at all of her books. Mom said she had to leave them. They wouldn't have space in the apartment. She would be able to read them when she came to visit her dad. But who knew when that would be? Would he even want to see his younger daughter? They'd barely said two words to one another her whole life. Unless he'd been drinking. Then he talked a lot.

It wasn't only the fear of a change of address that bothered Brody. She was starting middle school in the fall and the thought of not having her friends there with her scared her to death. She would have to go to the school downtown now. She had trouble breathing when she thought about it.

She walked over to her dresser and picked up the picture of Grandma Pat. Grandma would have said that God would take care of things; that she'd be all right. Brody wanted to believe that with all of her heart. But Grandma Pat was gone now. And it was growing harder and harder to remember the things she had taught Brody about God.

She closed her eyes and tried to pray, the way she and Grandma used to pray together. But she couldn't think of what to say.

Help me, Lord. I'm so scared.

It didn't seem enough.

So she just kept packing, placing all of her life inside a few cardboard boxes.

That night Brody dreamed that a huge wall surrounded her. It was made of very thick brick and was so high she couldn't see over it. She kept trying to scramble over the edge because she heard her family calling to her from the other side. Every time she jumped up she fell, crashing to the ground. But it never hurt because when she looked down, she saw that there were clouds underneath her feet. She tried to scale the wall, only to skin her knuckles painfully.

As she nursed her wounds, she heard the loveliest music. It came from the top of the wall. Looking up, she saw the most beautiful bird sitting majestically atop the brick. Where had she seen those eyes before? She lifted her hands and the bird flew to her. As the bird landed, it dematerialized and seemed to become one with her outstretched fingers. She looked down at her hands to see a rainbow of colors pass through her fingertips. This, too, soon disappeared and she was standing alone, on a bed of clouds, surrounded by a brick wall. She felt strengthened. Extraordinarily so.

"Brody!"

She pretended she did not hear her mother call. Quietly she slipped out the back door and ran up to the field. She was up in the apple tree before anyone could see her. From her perch she saw her mother look out the door and scan the hillside for her youngest daughter. Brody tried to make herself smaller and cringed into the camouflage of the surrounding branches and leaves.

It didn't work. Her mother began to slowly make her way up the hill. She panted slightly as she leaned in and peered up into Brody's hiding place. "Why are you hiding, Bro?"

Her voice was gentle, with only a hint of frustration. She knew how sensitive her daughter was. "You know we have to go. I told your dad we'd be gone before he got home from work."

Brody stared out over their small house and the surrounding territory. It looked so beautiful to her. "I know, Mom." She sighed heavily. "I guess I just wanted to say good-bye."

"This isn't for good, Brody. You can come back here anytime you want. You know that." Her mother reached up her hand to Brody. "Come," she simply said.

The girl took her mother's hand and obeyed.

Two

As Brody slept in her new bedroom that evening, Klaio's spirit left her for a time, ascending unto the Lord.

This child is so melancholy, my Lord, she chirruped. *There is no one for her. I fear my efforts will be for naught. There was one in her life who taught her of you, but that one is here with you now. There is no one in this child's life to steer her away from the peril her soul faces. Her father is an alcoholic. Her mother has seen too much pain to deliver her daughter from her own. Her brothers and sister are robed in their own grief. There is good there, yes...but no one to guide it. No one, Lord. No one. This child is alone.*

The Most High held out his hands and Klaio instantly flew to him. He wrapped His strength and His love around her. He breathed words over her. She felt His might run through her. She felt the joy of His Being. His words, unspoken, filled her heart.

There is one, Klaio. It will take some time and some

doing, but there is one. I will send this one to the child.

She was frightened. Things were changing too quickly. They had only been here two weeks and already the others seemed to belong.

Trina had made friends with some of the kids on the street. Brody liked these kids just fine but they scared her. Their parents were never around, and sometimes they used bad words. They stayed outside playing until well after dark. When Brody stayed with Trina during these times she noticed a strange look in her older sister's eyes. It reminded Brody of their mother's eyes. Always looking for something. Hungry.

As for Marshall, he was eating up this newfound freedom, as any ten-year-old boy would. Their mother trusted Brody and Trina to look after him while she was at school and work. Brody did her best, but Trina didn't seem worried when he went out combing the streets with some of the other boys. She had always followed Trina's lead before, hadn't she? Surely the boys weren't doing anything wrong. Probably just walking. She never asked Marshall.

Joshua was not there much of the time. It had been decided before the move that he would stay with dad. It was his junior year and he didn't want to change schools. Mom thought he was old enough to take care of himself. Besides, he had a girlfriend now. Brody missed him. Josh had always understood her the best.

The most difficult change for Brody to handle was the one that was taking place in her mother. Alicia Whitaker was doing the best she could. She just wasn't equipped for single parenthood. She had married their father when she was fifteen. She had no education or job skills. She was trying hard to change that. She had taken and passed her G.E.D. before leaving her husband. Now she was attending a government subsidized technical school that paid her minimum wage while she received secretarial training. During the day she worked long shifts at the SuperAmerica three streets down.

Their mother had always been the solid one. Whenever their dad was drinking, she made sure everything was okay. She was always there. Made sure they had everything they needed for school, tucked them into bed at night, read to them, played with them...in some ways she grew up with them. She'd had Joshua when she was seventeen years old. The other three came along every two years after that.

Alicia had always been a great mom. And now she wasn't there. Even when she was, she really wasn't.

There was this guy. Brody knew him from the bar her dad used to take them to. The kids would all sit in a booth and drink root beer and grape Nehi, while their dad and mom sat at the bar with their friends. This guy, Mike, was one of them.

Anyway, Mike was around a lot. And her mom didn't seem to care about anyone but him.

Brody spent most of the summer in the room she shared with Trina...reading. It was her only escape. Trina's new social circle made Brody painfully aware of her own awkwardness. Her sister's budding body made her self-conscious of her gangly pre-teen form. It seemed all the boys on the street were vying for Trina's attention. And Scotty was eighteen! He was the one Trina liked best. All of their gang would go to the empty lot down the street and hang out. Brody stayed in her room and read. She would usually hear the door slam around nine to tell her that her baby brother was out too.

She felt so alone. At night she would cry herself to sleep and she didn't even know why. This was not her world. She didn't belong here.

As the school year drew near she was filled with dread.

She knew deep inside of her that if she changed schools, her life would change forever. But then a voice whispered another possibility in her ear. A little chirruping voice. She knew it was her only chance. If only she could get her mother to agree.

"No."

Alicia's face was steeled against her daughter's pleas.

"Please, Mom, I'll be fine. I'll come and see you guys every weekend," Brody begged, panic seizing her. "I can't go to that school. Look at these kids on this street, Mom! I can't be like them! Please, Mom, please!"

The resolve on her mother's face wavered a bit. She saw it. "Your father...," she began, "he's never home. Who would watch after you? I just can't..."

"Josh will, Mom. We'll look after each other."

Her mother's face softened a little. She knew the two had been favorites since Brody was a baby. "Brody..."

"I'll watch him, Mom. You know you're worried about leaving him too."

"But he's almost seventeen! Brody, you're only twelve! Your dad doesn't know the first thing about taking care of a twelve-year-old girl."

"He'll never be there, Mom. You know that. I'll go to school and I'll come home. Nothing can happen to me there, Mom. You know that. NOTHING happens there. Can you say that about this place? Do you feel good when you leave us alone here?"

Brody looked away from her mother, ashamed at the truth in her words. It hurt her to be so bold, but she knew it was the only way her mom would listen. "I can't do this, Mom. I can't be like Trina...or...or any of these other kids around here."

Brody sought shelter in her mother's arms as she had all her life. But these arms felt different. These arms held her limply. In her mother's impassive embrace, Brody felt helplessness and defeat. So different from the arms of her early childhood. Those arms had been so strong and sure.

"All right."

It was mumbled into the top of Brody's head.

"What?"

"All right. You can go with him. But only for a year. By then I should be on my feet. We will be in a different place by then." Alicia held her daughter's chin in her hand. She looked directly into Brody's eyes. "If you ever need me, I'll always be here."

Brody nodded, tears readily trailing down her cheeks.

We did it, Lord. The child is away from temptation. Where we go now depends on her.

Are you so sure, Klaio?

Yes, my Lord. She will not reside in the center of Babylon, but with her father in her home.

Will it be her home, Klaio? He held out His hand and

the bird immediately lighted upon it.

What do you mean, my Lord? Klaio was genuinely concerned, for she had come to love the girl's gentle spirit.

It will not be the same, Klaio. This child's home has changed. It is an empty place.

She is a solitary child, Lord.

She chooses to be alone when many surround her. What will she choose when she is truly alone, Klaio?

I know not the answer, my Lord.

We will find it together, Klaio. We will find it together.

Three

Joshua gently shook his sister awake. "Come on, Bro. Time to get up. The bus comes in half an hour."

They ate their cereal in silence, each not knowing what to say to the other. It felt so strange to be just the two of them. What had always been a busy noisy kitchen now was silent, except for the echo of their spoons scraping the bottom of their bowls.

"Did Dad come home?"

She knew the answer before her brother shook his head. Should she worry? Did he care that it was their first day of school? Where could he be?

The calm of her brother busying himself at the sink soothed her. She knew where her dad was. Or at least what kind of shape he was in. There was no sense wasting her time worrying.

They grabbed their backpacks and raced out the door at the flash of lights in the distance.

She had been gone all summer. What did she expect? When she got on the bus she tried not to notice that Lara and Jenny were sitting together. Lara had been her best friend since kindergarten. But they hadn't spoken all summer. Her mother could not afford a telephone, and Brody had not known what to tell her friend about her parents' breakup anyway. She was still trying to figure it all out herself.

When Brody got on the bus the chatter between the two other girls stopped abruptly. She knew that they had been talking about her—about The Divorce.

Lara looked at Brody expectantly, but Brody pretended not to notice and quickly brushed past the two girls, plopping down into an empty seat a comfortable distance behind them. She swallowed hard as their whispering and giggling resumed a few minutes later.

It was the longest bus ride ever.

Middle school was different. So much bigger. And so many new faces. Most of the sixth graders, like Brody, weren't sure where to go. Teachers stood in the doorway and ushered them into the gymnasium.

Brody had never seen so many kids in all her life. The excited buzzing of all their voices filled the room and exploded in her ears. She wished Josh were here. Or Trina. Trina was supposed to show her around this place;

introduce her to all her friends. Miserably, Brody sat down on the first row of bleachers, unwilling to enter up into the sea of faces whirling before her.

When she turned around to sit down she came face to face with Lara, who was getting ready to climb up beside her.

Lara smiled quizzically.

"Why don't you sit with us, Bro? Come on up."

Jenny grimaced at Brody from behind Lara. She never had liked Brody.

"Oh, um, thanks, but I need to run to the restroom before the bell rings."

She was aware of the disappointment on Lara's face but didn't have time to wonder about it. She hurried off to the girls' locker room right behind the bleachers. Once inside, she threw her backpack on the floor and flopped down on a bench. It seemed so quiet in here compared to the crowded gym.

Brody buried her face in her hands and stifled a cry. She didn't know what to say to Lara. She didn't know what to say to anyone. She wasn't the same girl who had walked out of the elementary school last summer. She felt so alone.

Once she got the swing of her schedule Brody felt better about everything. She was taking some hard classes this year and the homework kept her pretty busy. Brody looked forward to the distraction. School was what she did best. She'd always been a straight A student, something of which her father was very proud. That was something anyway. Something she could do to please him.

The days seemed to crawl by. As soon as she got home from school Brody did her homework. Sometimes after that she would take walks in the woods. She loved to pick the wildflowers and give them names of her own making. Sometimes she would study the bugs under an upturned rock or peer into the stream for the ugly brown water snakes. Mostly she would just sit and listen to the sounds of the forest. Always, always she was thinking. Thinking of her mother...of Trina and Marshall. What were they doing? Were they okay? Wishing, wishing things were different. Then she would go home to her bedroom and read for hours until time to go to bed. She rarely saw her father. And Joshua was scarce these days too.

Her mother tried to call once a week. There was a pay phone outside of the convenience store where she worked. But sometimes two weeks would go by, sometimes three, before Brody heard from her family.

One weekend a month she and Josh would ride a different bus after school. It took them to their old elementary school. From there, they walked the seven miles to their mother's new apartment. Josh was always at least twenty feet ahead of Brody. He'd turn around occasionally and shout back to her to hurry up. He hadn't much patience for his little sister these days. Brody trudged on quickly under the weight of her backpack.

Their mother tried to be there to spend time with Brody and Josh when they visited, but most of the time she had to work. When she was home, they all went bowling or to the movies with Mike and his son.

Mike's son, Philip, was fifteen. Brody really didn't know him very well because he seemed painfully shy and rarely talked in the Whitaker children's presence. Brody felt sorry for him. She remembered his mom as a pretty lady with dark hair. She never seemed too happy to be at the beer joints. Brody didn't remember ever seeing Philip there. He stayed with his grandparents a lot.

On Sunday evenings Joshua's friend Nick would pick them up to take them back home. Usually the three of them would cruise through town so the guys could see if anything exciting was going on. Sometimes they would run into some of their friends and pull into an empty lot. Brody stayed in the backseat of the car, watching. She learned a lot from that backseat. The older girls pretended not to notice her: Josh's weird, wide-eyed, little sister. It wasn't long before she began to believe in the invisibility that began in that backseat.

18

Mostly Brody loved driving around with the two older boys. The loud music blaring in her ears from Nick's rear speakers filled her heart with its heavy beat. *Bum-bum. Bum-bum. Bum-bum.* All of her senses awakened at the vibrating bass line. Her eyes occasionally met with Nick's in the rearview mirror. His were usually curious. *He's wondering if I'm listening to all their talk about girls,* she thought. She always looked away. But then she would stare at the back of his head and wonder what it was like to kiss a boy.

It was a strange fall. A new world was opening up to Brody. With no one to talk to, she became ever more silent, settling in to her invisibility. It suited her grief over the loss of her family. Though there was always an ache in her heart, there was a strange joy as well. A new strength was growing inside her. She came to accept the unexpected. She came to look forward to her weekends in town. And the drive home after.

It was on one such Sunday evening drive home that she, Nick, and Josh ran into Carmen and Anne. Brody knew that Carmen was the girl Josh talked to on the phone for hours. Anne was Carmen's best friend. The two older girls squeezed in the front seat between the two boys. Brody didn't like the way Nick looked at Anne. She stayed in the backseat and turned her head away from the four that were quickly becoming two.

There was a whole group of high school kids now hanging out in the lot. The girls giggled loudly, and the boys pretended they didn't care. Different teens would poke their heads in the window to visit with the four in the front seat. Brody was watching a redheaded girl grab a guy's hat off his head when she heard Anne's voice.

"But what will we do with HER?" Anne pointed her chin in Brody's direction.

Brody tried to become even more invisible. But everyone was looking at her.

"Don't worry," said the redhead, popping up nearby. "She can stay with us. As long as you guys aren't gone all night anyway. I have to be home by midnight."

Before she knew what was happening, Brody was hustled out of the backseat of the car onto a flannel blanket that was laid out on the corner of the lot. All the older kids kept on doing what they had been doing as if they hadn't even seen the smaller girl. Brody watched as Carmen and Josh hopped in the backseat. Anne stayed glued to Nick's side even though she had more room now.

Josh turned to look at her briefly before slamming the door closed behind him. "We're going for a drive. We won't be gone long, Bro. Sierra will take care of you."

With that, he was gone. Brody watched as the

taillights made their way up the street. Away from her.

Brody sat very still and very quiet on the blanket the rest of the night. It was hard to be bored with so many people having fun around her. No one paid her any mind. The kids were just joking around, going from one car to the next and hanging out. Brody watched.

Suddenly a police car pulled in the lot. The flashing lights made her heart skip a beat. They would have to leave. The policeman said he would come back in twenty minutes. He wanted the lot empty when he returned.

As the black-and-white cruiser disappeared up the street, Sierra eyed Brody. "Now what am I going to do with you?"

The other kids were packing up their stuff to get going. Some were making plans to meet up at another place. Others had to be home to meet their curfews.

Sierra checked her watch. "Well, he said we had twenty minutes. Let's wait and see if your brother comes back any time soon." She plopped down on the blanket next to Brody.

Silence.

Sierra glanced over at Brody. "You don't talk much, do you?"

Brody felt her face grow warm but was saved from having to respond by a large white van pulling into the empty lot.

The two girls looked up. On the side of the van, in

large black letters, were painted the words: CHRIST'S TEMPLE. It was a church van. Brody realized they were across the street from some kind of church. They had been hanging out on church property.

Young boys began filing out of the van and running across the street to waiting vehicles. To Brody's horror, one of the figures looked vaguely familiar. She turned her head to hide her face, but as she did, she heard a whirring above her and looked up as a tiny bird flew about her head and then disappeared into the night. A bright pink feather floated down and landed in her lap.

"What the..."

She looked up and into Philip's puzzled face. *Darn that bird.*

"Brody?"

Sierra looked over at Brody. "Do you know this guy?"

Brody nodded.

"Good! Can you watch after her for a while? I've got to get home. It's almost midnight. My dad will kill me if I'm late again!"

With that, Sierra jumped up, grabbed her blanket out from under Brody, hopped into her tiny red car, and was gone.

Philip looked as if he might go into shock. Brody watched a tide of emotions wash over his face. From shock, to fear, to something akin to disgust, to pity, then...a mask. "Did Joshua leave you here with that girl?"

22

Philip knew her family's arrangement very well. Brody could only nod and look down.

Just then, the police cruiser pulled in beside them. "I thought I told you kids I want you out of here! Am I going to have to call your parents?"

"No, sir, there must be some misunderstanding. We're with a church group. We just got back from a youth mission trip. Our parents should be here any minute."

The policeman glanced at the parked church van but still eyed the two suspiciously. "Why don't you wait across the street then? This lot is becoming a hangout for some local kids, and I don't want anything to encourage that."

He watched until they reached the other side of the street before driving off again.

"Thanks." It was all she could think of saying, even though so many things were running through her mind.

"Where is your brother?"

Brody was surprised at his curt tone. "I don't know. He went for a drive with some of his friends."

"Carmen?"

Again, Brody looked down and nodded. Of course Philip had heard Joshua talk about Carmen.

"Did he say where they were going?"

"No."

"Did he say when they would be back?"

"No."

Philip took a frustrated breath. "You don't talk much,

do you?" he asked, exasperated.

Brody shrugged and looked away. She felt as if she might cry. Her lip began to quiver.

This time Philip looked away, sighing heavily. "Wait here."

She leaned against the metal fence surrounding the church play yard. He was walking toward an old station wagon with wood sideboards. She saw the window roll down. He was leaning in to say something. She saw him look over his shoulder in her direction. A face peered out at her.

It couldn't be. But Brody remembered that pale face and those dark eyes. It *was* his mother.

Brody's face turned red and she put her back between her and the station wagon. What would she do now? How could Joshua do this to her? Did anyone love her anymore?

An instant later Philip was beside her. He put his hand on her shoulder. "Brody."

She jumped. "What?"

"What did you learn tonight?"

"What?"

His face was red, and she could tell he was deliberately choosing his words. "What did you learn? One thing I've learned in life..." He paused and seemed to correct himself. "One thing I've learned is that you always have to look at what happens and decide what the lesson is. I mean, if the Israelites had learned from their first few mistakes they wouldn't have had to wander around in the desert for forty years, right?"

"What are you talking about?"

He sighed again. "Come on. Mom said she would wait here for a while to see if Josh comes back soon. If we sit in the car that cop won't bother us anymore."

Brody let him lead her to the car. Woodenly, she climbed in the backseat when he opened the door for her.

Philip's mom turned around to smile at her. Her eyes were really nice. "Hello, Brody, do you remember me?"

Brody nodded, looked away, and then, she couldn't help it...she looked back at the older woman and smiled. Something in her face made it okay. Something in her face made it actually feel good to be there.

Mrs. Pauley (was her name still Mrs. Pauley? Yes, of course it was. She hadn't remarried or anything...) made small talk with Philip about his church retreat. The boys had gone to the mountains and listened to several speakers preach about the spiritual responsibilities of today's youth.

Brody listened to mother and son discuss the merits and demerits of what he had experienced over the weekend. At first she was really interested in what they had to say. Then, slowly, she began to notice how they were connecting and the words that fell from their lips became meaningless. She watched as Philip's mother absentmindedly reached over and pushed a stray strand of hair from his eyes. He didn't even notice. He continued speaking excitedly, sharing everything he thought with his mother.

How she envied him. Something inside of her began to ache at the thought of someone, anyone to share her thoughts with...someone in whom to confide. Someone to trust. To trust that they would never change.

This boy wasn't shy. He definitely had no trouble talking about his thoughts and opinions. Why had she mistaken discomfort for shyness before? She could clearly see that this is where he belonged...where he could be himself. When he was with her and her siblings he must have felt like a fish out of water...like...like she did right now.

She must have sighed audibly because both sets of eyes in the front seat turned suddenly to look at her. One set was dark and sympathetic; the other, surprised to see her sitting there. Philip seemed to have forgotten about his unexpected charge.

Mrs. Pauley was apologetic. "I'm so sorry, Brody! Here we go on about these things when you must be worried about your brother. We'll wait five more minutes and then call your mom if he doesn't come."

"No! You can't do that! She doesn't have a phone, and besides, if Mom finds out...we'll both get in trouble. She might make me live with her and I...I couldn't stand that!"

Silence for a minute. Then, "I'm sorry, Brody. You and your family must be going through a very difficult time right now. I didn't realize that you weren't with your mother." She glanced reprovingly over at her son. "We'll wait a little longer."

They sat in silence for what seemed an eternity before Mrs. Pauley spoke again. "Brody?"

"Yes, ma'am?"

"Would you like to say a prayer? For your brother, I mean? I can tell you are worried about him."

Brody didn't know what came over her.

"If you don't mind, ma'am, could you pray for my whole family? Nothing's the same and everybody's different. I just want it back the way it used to be. I miss it so bad the way it used to be."

It was more words than she had pieced together in six months, but somehow Brody managed to get them out. Tears streamed down her face.

She took the smooth hand that was offered to her over the top of the seat. She was a little surprised when Philip offered her his hand as well. Then they prayed together. Just the three of them. When the prayers were done, Brody looked down at her hand and saw that she was still holding a bright pink feather in a death grip.

It's up to him now, Lord.

He will be an important part of her story, Klaio, but in the end it will always be up to her. By the way, that was quite an impressive flurry you demonstrated.

I couldn't help it, Lord. The boy was determined not to look at those two girls. He never would have seen Brody if I hadn't commanded his attention.

You are so right, Klaio.

She has one of my feathers, Lord.

And she will treasure it always, Beloved.

Four

They did not talk about what happened that night. The next morning Joshua averted his eyes as he pushed the Corn Flakes to her end of the table. She was too hurt to bridge the gap. She just didn't trust herself to bring it up. It was easier to believe he didn't care about her than to ask him why. "Why did you leave me for hours with strangers?" She wanted to scream it in his face. Her head was pounding as they boarded the bus. Very little sleep. So much sadness.

It had been a long week. She was looking forward to spending all weekend with her new library book. So when the phone call came...she was just as surprised as Josh. When he handed her the receiver with a mixture of annoyance and curiosity, she wanted to be snotty and smug. But she was much too shocked to be anything of the sort. She took the phone from his hand and held it limply for a moment before lifting it to her ear.

"Hello?"

"Brody?"

"Yes?"

"What have you learned this week?"

"What?"

A sigh.

"Mom wanted me to call you. She wanted me to ask if you'd like to go to church with us tomorrow."

Brody was confused. "Who is this?"

"It's Philip. Who do you think it is?"

"Oh! Ohhhhhhh." Of course. Who else would ask her something like that?

She started to politely refuse, then she looked up and saw Joshua eyeing her suspiciously. She turned her back to him and put on a voice that she hoped sounded sugary sweet.

"I'd love to go tomorrow! What time?"

There was a brief pause, as if Philip was surprised by her response. "Service starts at ten. Can you be ready by nine-thirty?"

"Sounds great. Do you know how to get here?"

"Yeah. Mom says she's been by there before."

Brody wondered when that might have been. It must have been back when their parents were all friends. "Okay then."

"Okay then, I'll see you then."

She looked up at Joshua defiantly. She couldn't resist. "Okay, then it's a date."

Click.

"Who was that?" Josh's tone was accusatory. He grabbed the phone roughly out of her hands.

"None of your business."

His face turned red.

"It is my business. Mom told me to look after you."

"Oh, ho-ho," she said sarcastically. "Look after me? *Look after me?* You mean like you did last weekend? Do I need to remind you about last weekend? Were you thinking about me when you drove off with Carmen? I don't think so. Don't even try to pretend you care about what happens to me, Joshua. You've already proven otherwise!"

At that she ran in her room and slammed the door and collapsed into a heap onto her bed. She was so mad. Big, fat, angry tears slid down her face as she buried it in her pillow. Her anger quickly dissolved, however, and was replaced by an emptiness that caused her body to shake with muffled sobs as she burrowed deeper into the pillow. She didn't want Josh to know she was crying.

She stilled herself resolutely at the gentle rapping on her door. Josh pushed the door open slightly and stood helplessly on the other side of the threshold. She rolled over and put her back to him.

"I'm sorry, Bro."

Her tears started anew at the pain in his voice, though she said nothing.

"I don't know why I did what I did last weekend. I just wanted to forget about it all. I wanted to forget about our family. I hate it, Bro. I hate what's happened to our family."

She could tell by his sniffles that he was crying a little too.

"I do care what happens to you, Bro. I care so much." His voice cracked but he said no more. He waited a few seconds, but when she said nothing he turned to leave.

"Josh?" She said it to the wall, too shy to let him see how much his words had meant to her.

He stopped abruptly and turned halfway around to face her back. "Yeah?"

"That was Philip on the phone. He wanted to know if I would go to church with him tomorrow."

She didn't really know what to expect. She'd never been to church before. The ones she'd seen on television shows had stained glass and ornate woodwork.

Christ's Temple had none of that. Philip explained during the drive in that their church used to be a high school. They were "blessed" with a gymnasium and large cafeteria, but the sanctuary itself was a bit uninspired. The school's small auditorium had been converted into its worship area.

Brody felt like she was getting ready to watch an educational film as she flipped the bottom of her seat down and nimbly lowered herself to a sitting position. Each row of seats was slightly higher than the one in front of it. She gazed down onto the tiny stage with a podium set up on it.

First, the preacher welcomed everyone and made a few announcements. Names that meant nothing to Brody. A lady in the hospital battling cancer. A man who was recovering from heart surgery. Someone's grandchild who was born premature. They all required prayer. And so it was provided.

They sang a song. Brody thought it beautiful but found it difficult to sing along, not knowing the melody. The people remained standing afterwards and recited something that Brody had never heard before. It was about what they believed. Brody glanced at Philip out of the corner of her eye. He was into it. Then she saw a smile tugging at the edges of his lips. He leafed around in the hymnal for a minute and shoved the book in front of her.

There it was! "I believe in God, the Father, Maker of heaven and earth and in Jesus Christ His only Son, our

Lord..."

She studied the words long after the congregation had finished saying them. An offering plate came around. Brody felt self-conscious that she had nothing to give. She noticed that Philip and his mother passed it along as well. They seemed neither uncomfortable nor ashamed. She pondered this a minute.

Wait! They were playing more music again! Everyone was standing up again. She looked at Philip wildly. He turned the page of the hymnal she still held. "Doxology," it was called. *Hmmm. Pretty.*

Another prayer. Suddenly, the lights dimmed. Brody's eyes searched the sanctuary frantically for clues as to what would happen next. Philip, sensing her unease, reached over and patted her hand kindly. Then he settled back into his seat as if preparing to watch a good movie.

The pastor approached the pulpit. Brody thought that he was young for a preacher. A few years older than her parents, she guessed. He wore wire-rimmed glasses and what looked like the beginnings of a goatee. His voice was kind and soothing.

Brody was so focused on taking everything in that she failed to listen to what the man was saying. She was too busy studying him and the people watching him. She was struck by the relaxed look on the faces surrounding her. She couldn't help noticing how they would nod when the preacher said something they agreed with or chuckle at his small jokes. For all practical purposes, those people were not here in the room with her. They were somewhere else...in the words of the sermon, carried away by the pastor's words. Even Philip was smiling knowingly.

Maybe I should be listening too, she thought. She struggled to catch the meaning of his sermon. He was speaking of obedience. *Children should be obedient to their parents. And we are all children of God.* Then he read the Scripture. Something in that Scripture struck her heart....spoke to her.

"Do not be afraid, Abram. I am your shield, your very great reward."

Brody felt those words sink down deep inside her. How long had she been afraid? She hadn't even been aware of it, yet these words made it so clear to her.

She had been afraid of losing her family. Afraid of losing her mother and Trina and Marshall. Afraid of Joshua growing up and changing. Afraid her father would never change. Afraid she would never matter; never mean anything to anyone.

Yet, here were these words spoken to her. God's words spoken to her through a promise to some guy named Abram.

She listened to the preacher tell Abram's story. His next words made her heart soar: "He took him outside and said, 'Look up at the heavens and count the stars—if

35

indeed you can count them.' Then he said to him, 'So shall your offspring be.'"

How often in the past year had she gazed up at the night sky dreaming she could take flight and soar above those heavenly bodies? How often had she looked up at God's sky and longed that He would scoop her up and take her away from her life?

Brody was one with the others now. She too was transported into the words that the pastor spoke. She had heard the story before. A long time ago. But as she pictured Abraham raising the knife to sacrifice his beloved, his only son, tears unashamedly streamed down her face. The story came to life in her mind. She understood the strong sacrifice Abraham had been asked to make. And he obeyed.

He left his family to follow the Lord. To search for a new land, a promise. How alone he must have felt! He must have been so afraid. Brody drew courage from this thought; the father of nations must have felt the same fears she was feeling right now.

"Do not be afraid. I am your shield, your very great reward."

Brody treasured these words and took them into her heart, making them hers. This was God's promise to her. And she believed.

That night, as she was laying her things out for school Brody felt that familiar anxiety. Facing the other kids had become extremely difficult. She couldn't figure out where she belonged anymore.

Not quite knowing why, she picked the bird up off her bureau top. She studied the beauty of its colorful surface, tracing each line and indentation gently with her finger. For some reason this small object brought her comfort. Clutching the cool hardness to her chest she quietly walked out onto the porch. Inhaling deeply she lifted her eyes to the night sky.

Klaio felt the child's sadness. Yet there was something different in this sorrow. The bird struggled to identify what the change was. Its pulse was fleeting but...there it went again...yes! Yes, that was it! Definitely. Brody Whitaker had found a small bit of hope.

"Look up at the heavens and count the stars—if indeed you can count them," Brody remembered. Then she began to pray.

Lord? God! Show me what to do. I'm so scared. I'm so lonely, Father. I just want things back the way they were!

Brody dropped her head at this thought. She knew her life would never, never be the same again. She rubbed the bird with her thumb.

Please take care of Marshall, Father. He's still so young. Mom is so lost. She doesn't realize how much he needs her. And Trina...don't let her do anything bad, Father. She needs Mom too. She just doesn't know it. And Josh is so angry. He blames Mom for everything. It seems like he hates her!

She looked up at the stars once again. The sky was so big—so vast and wide. Could God really hear her down here? She felt so small and insignificant. She sighed and sat down on the steps.

And Mom. I don't know what to pray for her, Father. I miss her so much. But even when we are together it seems like she's not there. Where did she go? Why do things have to change? Help us, Father! Please!

She buried her face in her hands and cried for a little while. Then she got up and went to bed.

Five

The murmur of voices became background noise as Brody stared out the school bus window. She pressed her forehead firmly against the glass. The rain pelted the window and colored the rest of the world gray. But she didn't notice. Her mind was full of a rainbow of thoughts. She kept hearing the preacher's voice in her head. She kept seeing the stars swimming above her. She kept seeing Philip's mother brushing the strand of stray hair from his eyes.

"Do you care if I sit with you?"

Brody looked up, startled, into Lara's anxious face. "No...sure, I mean, go ahead."

Brody wondered where Jenny was today. As if reading her mind, Lara spoke up quietly. "Jenny has some kind of stomach bug. I'm supposed to get her homework. Anyway—" the girl paused uncomfortably—"anyway, I'm kinda glad because I've been wanting to talk to you."

Oh no. Here it comes, thought Brody. *The sympathy talk. Sorry about your parents, blah, blah, blah.* She braced herself.

"I just wondered..." Lara's voice sounded really small. "I just wondered why you are mad at me. I mean, I know you're going through a lot of stuff, but I thought we were best friends."

To her surprise, Brody saw tears forming around the edges of Lara's eyes. For the first time she realized how selfish she had been. Didn't she owe her best friend a little more than she had been giving?

"I'm not mad at you, Lara! I just...I just didn't think you wanted to be my friend anymore. And I just feel weird around everyone now that...now that..." Brody couldn't finish what she was trying to say.

"I don't care if your parents are getting a divorce! I mean, I'm sorry for you and all, but it doesn't change the fact that you're my best friend. I just wish you'd talked to me instead of shutting me out."

The bus jerked to a stop in front of their school. The kids filed off and scurried into the building, pulling jackets and backpacks over their heads to try to fend off the rain. When they got under the patio roof the girls stared at each other awkwardly for a second. When the bell rang they each started off into opposite directions.

"Ask your dad if you can come over tomorrow night," Lara shouted over her shoulder. "We're having a marshmallow roast!"

"He doesn't care what I do," Brody responded without

thinking. Still she tried to control the happy feeling that was bubbling up inside her as she headed to her homeroom.

She rode her bike the three miles to Lara's house at breakneck speed. She couldn't wait to see her friend and talk like they used to.

Lara lived on a farm. Her family was always mucking out some barn or breaking in some horse or baling the hay. Brody loved to be with them. There were five kids. Lara had an older brother, Dean, who was Trina's age. Trina had had a crush on him for years. Lara's older sister, Leah, was the same age as Josh. They were friends, but not close. Leah was an intellectual and played the piano. Then there were the two younger sisters: Jane and Carrie. Jane was the same age as Marshall. Only Carrie had no counterpart in their family. *Thank goodness,* thought Brody. *That would be one more body to worry about right now.*

The Spence kids were incredibly normal. Brody almost felt normal when she was with them. They talked to each other and played together. They worked together and occasionally fought. But they LIKED each other.

Mr. and Mrs. Spence really seemed to enjoy spending

time with their children. They laughed and joked around with them a lot. Because she was so shy, the whole Spence family teased Brody mercilessly when she was there. One time when she stayed for dinner, they served deer meat and told her it was steak. She didn't understand why they all stared at her when she took the first bite. Then they all laughed and asked her if she liked it. They just didn't understand that she would have eaten a cardboard box just to be with them, to be part of their family for a little while.

Then there was the time when she stepped in the cow manure...they all laughed about that one to this day. Their whole family seemed to enjoy bringing her out of her shyness. Brody smiled to herself as she thought about it.

As she coasted down the last hill, Lara's house came into view. Brody's smile turned into a frown as soon as she looked up. There in the yard was Lara. And standing right beside her was Jenny.

Brody pulled into the driveway and hopped off her bike. Both of the other girls ran up to greet her.

Brody tried to make her voice sound glad.

"I thought you were sick!" she said to Jenny.

"I'm over it," Jenny responded. "It was only a twenty-four-hour thing. I really didn't want to miss Lara's marshmallow roast."

Brody couldn't help thinking that Jenny sounded a little snotty. She looked at Lara, who was smiling a little apologetically.

"Yeah, Jenny called me this morning and said she felt well enough to come. Isn't that great?"

"Yeah!" Brody tried to sound enthusiastic, but she felt her heart sink. She would have to share Lara all night.

Oh, well, that little twittering voice inside her head said. *It'll be okay. You may even find that you like Jenny too.*

Brody sure didn't feel like it would be okay. She glanced over at Jenny. The girl looked tired. She felt a little wave of sympathy. Maybe it would be okay after all.

It turned out to be one of the best nights Brody would ever remember. She and Lara fell right back into a comfortable companionship. Even Jenny seemed friendly. The other Spence kids each had a friend over as well, so there was quite a crowd around the campfire that evening. Mrs. Spence led everyone in singing some old camp songs. She had a really pretty voice. Mr. Spence played the guitar and sang at the top of his lungs. Brody's face was warm from the fire and from happiness. They made s'mores and caught lightning bugs and played freeze tag in the dusk. She was careful not to step in cow manure.

That night the three girls talked long into the night. Brody forgot about any distance she had ever imagined between herself and Lara. But it was Jenny who surprised her.

It had all started when Lara asked, "How's your mom doing?"

It seemed like an odd question. After all, how many kids their age even knew much about their friends' parents? But Brody sensed that this was more than just a polite "how do you do."

"She's really sick this week." Jenny's voice sounded hollow in the dark. "Her doctor said the new medicine would make her that way for a while."

Mrs. Spence stuck her head in the door. "Girls, go to sleep, or we'll have to separate you. I don't want to hear any more giggling, okay?"

"Okay," came the chorus of responses.

Brody couldn't stop herself from asking. "What's wrong with your mom?" she whispered.

"She has cancer. She's had it for five years now. This is the worst she's ever been. Dad says it's because the medicine is working. See, to kill the cancer, it has to make other parts of her sick too. But those parts will get better. Only the cancer will die."

Brody was taken aback by the hopelessness in Jenny's voice. Five years. Jenny's mom had been fighting cancer since Jenny was six or seven years old. Brody swallowed hard and tried not to think of losing her own mother.

"I hope it works," Brody said. Her voice came out all raspy. She hoped that Jenny couldn't hear the fear in it.

"It will," Jenny said firmly. "It has to."

"What have you learned this week, Chicken?"

His voice came out loud and cheerful on the answering machine. And why did he call her "Chicken"? Hardly a flattering nickname.

"We'll pick you up tomorrow at the usual time. There's a luncheon after church so...bring your appetite!"

Brody found herself smiling at his voice. She missed him, she guessed. But she would never tell him that.

What had she learned? She thought about her sleepover at Lara's last night. And about Jenny. And about Jenny's mom.

I learned that true friends stick by you no matter what, she thought. *And I learned that people are not always what they appear to be. Sometimes they hide their fear and pain behind ugliness. Sometimes you have to try a little harder to find out the truth.*

Maybe I'll call Jenny tonight, she mused. *Maybe I'll ask her if she wants to come to church tomorrow.* There was that voice again.

Jenny was smiling. And Brody was glad she had asked her to come. She could tell that Philip hadn't known what to think this morning when two girls hopped into the back of the station wagon instead of just one. But he had beamed when she introduced her friend to him and his mother. Now they were all having lunch, sharing a table with a blue-haired lady and a woman with two young daughters.

Jenny had made friends with the little girl, who looked to be about two years old. The older girl's hair fascinated the child. Jenny had beautiful blond strands that curled into corkscrews and cascaded about her heart-shaped face. The child kept grabbing a curl, pulling it taught, and then letting it go to watch it bounce like a spring back to where it started.

"This is Desiree," Jenny told Brody, face shining. "But everyone calls her Desi."

Jenny's eyes took on a distant look and she said, more to herself than to Brody, "I always wanted a little sister...but..."

She turned back to the child and began talking to her in a high-pitched voice.

Brody turned away. She was looking for Philip. When she finally caught sight of him, she noticed that he was staring at Jenny from the dessert line. Something about the look on his face made her heart sink. She took a drink and walked outside.

Stepping into the church's courtyard was like entering Paradise to Brody. In the center of the building, surrounded by glass, the garden boasted roses of all colors and sizes. Even though it was fall, the flowers still thrived voluminously under the loving care of church volunteers. In the brilliant sunlight of midday, the reds and pinks were so vibrant that Brody grew dizzy looking at them. She withdrew to a small bench that was shaded by a climbing rose and supporting lattice. She sat down and breathed in deeply the heady perfume of the flowery atmosphere.

Why should she care? So what if Philip did like Jenny? It wasn't like she liked him or anything. So why did it hurt so much? Brody fought back tears at the thought. She was just so tired of being second best. All of her life everyone liked Trina best. No one ever noticed the quieter younger sister. And now…just when she was learning to like Jenny….

Why, Lord? She couldn't stop herself from asking the question. *Don't you think I'm special too?* The tears slid readily down her face at her imagined rejection.

Then she heard it.

The song was so beautiful. So strange, yet oddly familiar. It came from a dense shrubby growth of roses in the corner of the patio. She was sure she had heard that song before. But where? Brody only knew a few birds. Grandma Pat had taught her some. Just the regular ones:

47

robin, cardinal, house sparrow...she didn't even think she could recognize their songs. But she knew this one.

Transfixed, she walked toward the bush. The song grew more melodic, more inviting. Brody didn't know what she was doing, but she was drawn to the music. And then, something amazing happened. She began to hear words. A whole chorus of the most beautiful voices arose from the rose bush. The words were plain as day in her mind...but it was unlike anything she had ever heard in her life.

The king is enthralled by your beauty; honor Him, for He is your Lord...

Clothed with splendor, wrapped in light...

Great is His love, higher than the heavens;

His faithfulness reaches to the skies...

Take refuge in the shelter of His wings,

Find comfort in His love...

"Brody?"

The door banged loudly shut behind him. She heard a rustle in the leaves and the music was gone.

"What are you doing, Chicken?"

Brody forced a laugh and tried hard not to be angry with him. "Would you puh-leeze stop calling me that!"

"I like it. It suits you."

"Thanks a lot," she said, sarcastically. Then, "Philip?"

"Hmmm?" He was eating a fistful of peanuts and kept popping them in, one by one.

"Did you hear some music...just now? I mean, right before you came out here?"

"Uh-uh. Why?"

She tried not to look too disappointed. Her hands were itching to dig into the bush and see if anything was there.

"Oh, nothing. I just thought I heard this song, that's all."

"What did it sound like?"

"Oh, I don't know. It said something about taking shelter under God's wings or something."

Philip shrugged. "Maybe the choir is practicing."

He opened the door and, indeed, Brody heard a choir of voices come from within the building. But those were not the voices she had heard.

"Maybe."

"Would you and Jenny like to come over for dinner?"

That night she combed her Bible for the words of the song. She couldn't remember them all so that made it kind of hard. Then she stumbled onto the book of Psalms. So many beautiful words. The part about the king being enthralled by her beauty was in chapter forty-five, verse eleven. She cried when she read it.

How had He known?

At the very moment that the voices had started singing Brody had felt like the ugliest girl in the world. How had He known?

She read through the rest of the book. Her Bible was old. It had belonged to Grandma Pat. Several pages fell out in her hands as she turned them. She was disappointed to discover that Psalm 54 through 102 was missing. What could have happened to those precious chapters? She looked all over for the part about taking shelter under His wings. She felt sure it must be somewhere in the book of Psalms.

She fell back onto her bed, clutching her Bible to her chest.

What was she thinking? Did she really believe that she had heard the voices of angels? That had to be the choir that she'd heard. But in her heart she knew it was not.

How did you convince the heavenly host to go to that rose bush, Klaio?

His voice was very stern and Klaio shivered at the thought of His wrath.

They love the child, Lord, she replied.

Of course they love the child, Klaio. She is my daughter. The Lord sighed and His light filled the sky. *You must stop these interventions, Klaio. I know that you pity the child. I know that you love her. Her soul is very gentle. She has the heart of David. But...if you insist on these tactics, we shall be working with her from a mental institution, do you understand? We must work on her faith, not with visible acts.*

Yes, my Lord.

Klaio heard the love in His voice, behind the rebuke. *Lord?*

Yes, Klaio?

Is there still much suffering ahead?

There is still much to learn, Klaio, my love. There is still much to teach.

Every Sunday after church Brody, Jenny, and Philip would hang out and then eat dinner with his mom. Sometimes they went to the mall, other times the pool, the park, wherever their hearts would take them on that particular day. Sometimes Lara would come. Those were the best days for Brody. On those days she didn't feel like a third wheel. But Lara's family went to another church, so she rarely joined the threesome on their Sunday adventures.

They were three friends all hiding from something, all running away. Brody was running away from an empty house, Philip from loneliness, and Jenny...Jenny was running from fear. Being home to her meant being afraid that her mother would die. Being home meant seeing the frightened look in her father's eyes. Being home meant watching her mother waste away. She was forgetting that her mom had ever been any other way but sick.

Philip was great for Jenny. He obviously liked the girl a lot. His teasing seemed to make Jenny forget her troubles. She seemed to like Philip too.

As time went on, Jenny's mother grew more and more ill. Brody felt fiercely protective of Jenny. She had lost her family, but she still was able to visit them. She couldn't imagine losing them for good. Her heart ached for her new friend. Everyone knew it was just a matter of time.

On the day that they buried Jenny's mother Philip and Brody stood on either side of their friend, holding her up as the sobs racked her body. Neither one would let her go. Neither one would let her fall to the ground. They watched as the long black car carried Jenny and her dad away. Jenny's voice would ring in their ears for a long time after.

"Why? Why would He let her die? I've prayed so hard. Why, why, why?"

Later that evening at Philip's, he and Brody shared a root beer in silence.

They sat on lawn chairs and stared out at the dirty streets.

"What did you learn today, Chicken?"

His voice sounded old, like he neither cared, nor would he believe whatever Brody's response would be.

Somehow it broke her heart to know his spirit was so grieved. She reached over and took his hand in hers.

"I learned," she said softly, looking down at their hands intertwined, "I learned that we can never understand God's ways. And I learned that there is strength in friendship. There is strength in love."

He swallowed hard and squeezed her hand a little before pulling his free. "No," he said. "We can never understand. His ways are too great for us to understand."

Although his voice was a whisper, Brody heard and understood. And though her heart was troubled for her friend too, she knew that they would all be okay. For the first time in her life, she knew that they would all be okay.

Six

As much as she missed her mother and her two other siblings, it was always hard on Brody to visit them. She felt like an alien when she was in their world. Today was no different.

As soon as she entered the apartment Trina pulled her into their room, smiling secretly.

"I have to tell you something," she said, in an excited tone.

Brody smiled. She had forgotten how fun it was to be around her older sister. Her mood was always contagious.

"What? What is it?" Brody calmly began unpacking her bag but the corners of her mouth tugged upward.

"I have a boyfriend!"

Surprise, surprise.

Brody flopped down onto the bed and put her hands behind her head. "Do tell," she said smartly.

Trina giggled and bounced down onto the foot of the bed. "It's Scotty, Bro. I finally got him to notice me. We were at this party last night and he finally kissed me and stuff."

Trina's cheeks looked a little flushed.

Brody raised her eyebrows. "And stuff?"

Trina looked away quickly and flopped over on her back beside Brody. "Oh, you know, just a lot of kissing and stuff."

Then the tone of her voice changed and she sounded so happy. "Oh, Brody, I like him so-o-o much!"

Brody didn't know what to say to Trina. Something about the way her sister was swooning over this guy worried her. She knew how Trina could get when she wanted something.

"That's great, T. Just...just be careful, ok? He's so much older."

"Only four years. That's not much. I just wish we had a telephone! I'm so sick of walking to that payphone any time I want to talk to him!"

"Well, you get to see him at the lot, don't you? Do you guys still hang out there?"

"Only at night. And I want to talk to him all day long!"

Brody smiled at Trina's silliness. She got up and started unpacking her bag.

"Oh, yeah, Bro?"

"Ummm-hmmm?"

"There's something else I almost forgot to tell you, but you have to pretend you're surprised when Mom tells you, OK?"

Brody continued with her unpacking. "What?"

"Mom's going to have a baby. We're getting another little brother or sister."

"What did you just say?" Philip's face was incredulous.

"It's true. We're going to have a baby brother or sister."

He slammed his fist down hard on the table in front of him. "How could they do that? I mean, how could they be so stupid!"

Philip's anger surprised Brody. She'd never seen him lose control this way. "Well, I don't think they planned it, if that's what you mean."

"Doesn't this bother you? They're not even married, Brody! What they did was wrong."

"Nothing I say or think will change anything. I know my mom and dad will never get back together now. Do you think that makes me happy? Besides, doesn't the Bible say we should spend less time criticizing people and more time loving them? My mom needs me to love her right now. I could tell by the look in her eyes that she doesn't know what's going to happen when this baby comes. She's scared, Philip."

Philip walked over to the window in the small living room of his mother's house. His eyes followed the cars driving by on the city street. His shoulders drooped a little and he dropped his head to his chest. Brody sensed a change come over him.

"Take the plank out of your own eye..."

"What?"

Philip's voice was distant and he seemed to be staring off at nothing. Then he turned back to Brody. The look on his face was not happy; rather, it was determined. "You're right, Chicken. Sometimes The Plan is unclear to us." He shrugged. "I always wanted a little brother."

"And what if it's a little sister?"

Philip ruffled her hair affectionately. "I already have one of those."

She was back in her own room. It was late, but she was having difficulty falling asleep. Josh was out with his friends. Only heaven knew where Dad was.

Brody picked the bird up and gazed at it in the moonlight streaming through her window. *Where would you fly, little one? If your wings were feather light instead of anchors at your sides, where would you fly?*

She rubbed the stone with her thumb. To her

surprise, it felt like silk under her skin. Not knowing why, she pressed Klaio to her lips and felt the coolness quiet her insides.

She closed her eyes and tried to pray but felt unsure of the words.

*I meant what I said to Philip today, Lord. I know that just wishing for something will not make it happen. If that were so, my family would be back together and happy. I know this baby means an end to this possibility, Lord. When my dad finds out...*she drew in a deep breath at the thought...*when he finds out he will be very hurt. And very angry.* She squeezed her eyes shut tighter. *I don't know what to hope for anymore. My mom is starting a new family now. Marshall will no longer be the baby.*

Her thoughts moved to her little brother. He had taken her for a walk downtown yesterday. Wanting to show off his newfound toughness, he led her inside a department store. Just goofing off at first, he strutted around the aisles like he owned the place. When suspicious sales people began to watch them cautiously, he pretended to look through the racks of clothes. When the saleswomen were looking the other way, he spit great big goobers on piece after piece. She had giggled at his disrespect because she knew that was what he wanted her to do...but later she had cried. He scared her.

What is happening to my baby brother, Lord? Who will look after Marshall?

The tears slid down her cheeks and bathed Klaio in their dewy softness. This would not be the last night that Brody would cry herself to sleep.

Seven

What was that noise?

Brody glanced into Joshua's room but was unable to tell if he was home yet. She glanced at her clock. *2:00 a.m.*

There it was again! Someone was trying to get in the door. Either Josh forgot his key, or dad couldn't get it together enough to unlock the door.

She sighed heavily and went to help. Just as she entered the hallway, a large man burst through the door with Brody's dad, J.D., hanging off his shoulder. The man was staggering under J.D.'s weight. Brody stayed hidden in the shadows.

The man staggered over to the couch and dumped J.D.'s body onto the cushions. As he passed by her hiding spot, the smell of alcohol nearly knocked Brody over. She wrinkled her nose in disgust.

The man sat down on the couch at J.D.'s feet.

Brody tried to remain invisible. The way her father's body looked frightened her. It seemed so still and lifeless.

Was he okay?

She leaned in a little farther to try to see his face. Was he breathing? She accidentally brushed against the hall table.

Crash! A picture fell to the floor.

The man stood up. "Who's there?" He walked slowly toward the hall.

Brody backed away from his approaching figure, closer to her bedroom door.

The man's face leered through the doorway. When he caught sight of Brody, his mouth spread into a slow smile.

Brody was suddenly aware of her long legs sticking out from under her nightshirt. She crossed her arms over her chest in an attempt to hide her tiny body.

"Hello, sweetheart."

Brody cringed at the sound of his voice. There was something about it that she didn't like.

He walked forward. "Do you live here with 'ol J.D.?"

As he came toward her she began to back away.

"Don't worry darlin', I'm not gonna hurt you." His tone was soft, like he was trying to tame a wild animal. He stretched out his hand toward her. "What do you got there?"

Looking down, Brody realized she still clutched the bird tightly in her hand.

He reached out and touched her hair. "Such a pretty little girl," he said softly.

She flinched and pulled away, but it was too late. The man pulled her arm roughly and began to push her backward through her bedroom door. She struggled furiously, but that only seemed to make his hold grow rougher. The smell of him made her gag. She tried to scream, but no sound would come from her mouth. She tried to break away, but that only made him laugh, a low gurgling chuckle that seemed to come from deep inside his chest.

When he pushed her back on her bed, she found her voice. "Daddy! Help, Daddy, help!" She screamed at the top of her voice, but it only came out a feeble little yell.

The man just laughed harder. "Your daddy can't hear nothin', sugar. He ain't a-gonna wake up for a long time."

She screamed again. This time it angered the man, and he lifted his hand and slapped her hard across the face. It was strange that she couldn't feel the pain.

"I said ain't nobody gonna hear you, so just shut up your yellin'," the man said viciously.

Her world began to fade. She clutched the bird to her heart and turned her head away from his stench.

As Klaio touched Brody's heart, she flew. She flew into Brody's heart and saw the girl's terror. She saw Brody's shock and inability to react. In an instant the bird knew it was up to her. Invisible to eyes from this world, she flew quickly into the next room, where Josh was sleeping.

With no sound at all she fluttered around his head, fanning him with her feathers until he was batting his arms about in his sleep. She watched as he began to wake up....

Josh woke to what sounded like the whirring of wings and heard strange noises coming from the room across from his. He jumped out of bed, listened at the door a moment, then sprang into action. Grabbing something from his closet, he flew into the other room.

"Get away from my sister, you pig!" Josh ordered.

The man turned around slowly and stared into the barrel of a shotgun. He froze. "Put that down, son. You don't wanna get hurt."

Josh held the gun steady, his eyes a steely gray. "Get out of this house, you scumbag, before I send you where you deserve to go."

"All right, all right." The man raised his hands and slowly stood to his feet. He backed away from Brody and out the door.

Josh followed him, gun steadily aimed at his head.

Brody's head ached. She could feel her eye begin to swell where the man had struck her. She heard the door lock and shortly thereafter an engine start up and slowly fade off in the distance. Only then did she begin to cry.

Josh came in with an ice pack and placed it gingerly on her eye. She lifted her hand to hold it in place. Josh put his arms around her. Her whole body was shaking. At last she was safe in her big brother's arms.

"Brody, Brody, Brody...I'm so sorry. I'm so sorry." His voice was laced with pain. "Are you okay? Did he...?"

Brody shook her head but still couldn't find her voice.

"I have to call the police, Bro. I can't let that guy go." Joshua made a move to get up.

Brody panicked when she felt his arms leave her. "Don't leave me, Josh! Please don't leave!"

He sat back down, put his arms around her trembling body, and held her.

As Brody finally drifted off to sleep, she realized she was still holding the bird close to her heart.

Klaio, Klaio, Klaio...what will I do with you, my love?

I'm so sorry, My Lord. I felt her fear. I could not ignore it. Punish me if you must. I did not mean to be deliberately disobedient."

The Lord held out his hand. The bird flew to Him. He pressed His lips into the bird's soft feathers. *I love you, Klaio. I love your heart.*

Klaio felt His tears cleanse her, and she knew that she was forgiven.

Brody could hear the yelling before she opened her eyes.

"Just go look at her, Dad! Go see for yourself what you did!"

Brody heard her father mutter an expletive and get up from the couch. She closed her eyes again and feigned sleep. She heard his footsteps through the hallway and felt his presence in her doorway.

J.D. drew in a sharp breath. He muttered something under his breath before he turned away. Brody opened her eyes and watched his back retreat into the living room.

Slowly she got up and moved to her bureau. The face staring back at her was foreign to her. She raised her hand and felt the puffiness of the left side of her face. Her left eye was swollen shut and discolored.

Brody crossed her arms around herself, trying to block out the memory of last night. Her arms were tender where the stranger's hands had been. Fear coursed through her body.

What if he came back?

She heard Joshua's voice.

"I'm calling the police. If you don't even know who brought you home last night you are a pitiful son-of-a..."

Joshua's voice trailed off, his anger dissipating into hopelessness. "Don't you even care? Don't just sit there like that! Don't you even care what your drinking has done to our family?"

She heard her dad shift angrily in his seat.

"Don't talk to me like that. I'm your father!"

Hearing Joshua move suddenly, she knew what was going to happen. She ran into the living room. "Josh, no!"

Her brother was on top of their father, his hands squeezing their father's throat. She tried to pull him off. She could feel the tension in his muscles, the restraint alongside the violence.

At her touch, Joshua roughly withdrew his hands from their father's neck. There were tears of rage in his eyes as he stared at the man rubbing his neck painfully.

The boy looked down at his hands almost fearfully. "I don't even know you!"

He ran from the house and slammed the door behind him.

Brody sat on the floor, a few feet from where her father still was gasping for air. She stared at the now-closed door, filled with despair.

J.D. began to sob, cradling his head in his hands. He crawled over beside Brody and searched for her hands. "I'm so sorry, baby. I never meant to hurt you. I never wanted anyone to be hurt. Not you, not Josh...not your mom..." He was grasping her hands and speaking between sobs. He reached up and gently stroked her swollen face. "I'm so sorry...I'm so sorry..."

She put her arms around him. "It's okay, Daddy. It's going to be okay..."

J.D. had been asleep for two hours when Joshua finally returned home. Brody was sitting at the kitchen table drinking a cup of tea. Josh came over and put his hands on her shoulders.

"I'm sorry I left you. I was afraid...I was afraid I was going to kill him."

She put her hand on top of his. "I know. It's okay."

He sat down across from her and held her hand. His eyes searched hers earnestly. "I know his name, Brody. I went to all the bars dad goes to. I finally found the last one. The bartender knew him. He remembered who drove him home. I went to the police, Brody. This guy is already in trouble, Bro. They've been looking for him for awhile."

Her brother hesitated and looked down at their

fingers intertwined. "I need to know, Bro...do you want to be involved in this? Can you identify this guy? Because if you don't want to..."

Brody closed her eyes as the man's face loomed before her in her mind. She could smell the stench of his sweat and alcohol. She felt her stomach lurch. Quickly she got up and ran to the bathroom.

Joshua followed her. He held her hair and rubbed her back as she threw up. His face was a mask of concern and determination when she turned to face him again.

"I'm sorry, Bro. I know this is hard...I thought I was doing the right thing...I don't want that pig walking around..."

Brody took a deep breath. Her voice came out as a whisper. "It's okay, Josh. You're right, I know. I just need...a little...just need some time to think."

She put her hand to her head. It was beginning to ache again.

He put his arms around her. Safety. "I know. I know."

I have failed her, my Lord.

You and I both know what would have happened had you not awakened the young man, Klaio.

Yes, Lord, but I should have seen this coming! Why did you shield it from me, my Father? I could have...

What would you have done, Klaio? Have you not learned anything from the broken hearts of history? Suffering brings with it change, Klaio. You yourself know this to be truth. You have witnessed it many times. A broken heart is the greatest of all teachers, the greatest instigator of change.

But what must the child change, my Lord? She is sweet and pure of heart. Her eyes see like David's...forgive me, my Lord, for I am grieved. What would you have this gentle one become?

The Lord held out His hand and the bird flew to Him. He breathed the breath of life onto her wings, giving flesh to her grief. She watched as it rose above her in a whirlwind of colors. Like a tiny hurricane it swirled around and around, seeming to grow larger as the seconds passed. Then it disappeared.

I was not speaking of the child when I spoke of change, my Love.

Eight

When she had packed everything seemed so small. Nothing mattered. Only to leave. And to leave behind the pictures that invaded her dreams every night.

She left her books. Her journal. Her pillow. She left her friends without saying good-bye. She hadn't been back to church with Philip since. She left Joshua. Her father. And, of course, she left Klaio.

The tiny bird reminded her of that night. But it had been a decision she regretted. She missed the coolness of the stone in her hand, the warmth in her heart when she held the bird. The loss of this beloved object was only a small part of the emptiness inside of her now. She would never go back to her father's house, she thought. Fear gripped her when she imagined it.

You are lucky, she tried to tell herself. *So much more could have happened. Joshua saved you.*

But her heart was broken.

She changed schools without batting an eye. She walked through the halls of Central Middle School like a ghost. No one knew her and no one noticed her. She willed herself invisible.

She did her work faithfully. She watched her mother's tummy grow and exclaimed over its roundness. She laughed at Marshall's antics. She listened intently to Trina's lovesick declarations. But all the while she felt she was dying inside.

Only Josh knew the truth as to why she had moved back with their mom. They both agreed that until the man was behind bars they did not want Brody in the hollow. Josh decided to stay because there were only a few months of school left. Neither one wanted to worry Alicia. Their mother simply thought that Brody had had a change of heart, that she had missed her mother and siblings too much to stay away any longer.

This was true, of course. Brody had never needed her mother more in her life than she did at this time. Unfortunately, Alicia had so many things to attend to that she failed to notice her daughter's withdrawn behavior.

Brody never left the house. She always had a good reason. Homework. Reading a good book. Tired. Headache. Neither Marshall nor Trina seemed to question. Brody had always been a bookworm. It did not seem strange to them at all.

Philip seemed to know that something was wrong. He would not give up. He could not accept Brody's sudden disinterest in church and God.

When Brody's mother finally got a telephone, he called every day.

"What have you learned today, Chicken?"

"Nothing new, Philip."

"There must be something, Chicken."

There would be a long pause as Brody swallowed hard and searched for something witty to say. So she began to make things up. Silly things to make him smile and maybe forget what she used to be like.

"I learned there are seven stop signs on the way home from school." Or, "sewer rats do not prefer Taco Bell." Or "all of the profane graffiti on the retaining wall seems to be written by a left-hander." Or some other such nonsense. And Philip, who was left-handed, would laugh, but she felt his worry grow deeper.

One day he grew tired of the game and was unable to hide his irritability. "Tell me something real, Bro. Tell me what you think. Tell me what you feel."

Her voice was very quiet when she spoke but the conviction in her tone caused him to catch his breath.

"I learned that it's a sick world out there, Philip."

"What do you mean?"

"Ugly things happen every day, and no one even knows about it."

"What kind of ugly things, Chicken? What are you talking about?"

A long pause.

"Oh, you know...like people using aerosol spray cans instead of pumps. That crap'll ruin the atmosphere, you know."

"Come to church with us Sunday, Bro. Everyone

misses you."

"I can't. I've got a paper I really have to work on."

"You shouldn't put anything before the Lord."

"Pray for me then."

"What should I pray?"

"Whatever you want to."

After that he went to see Joshua. And everything became crystal clear.

"She has Post-traumatic Stress Disorder."

"She has what?" Joshua said.

"The elders from our church did some mission work with abuse victims and we had some training on how to handle it. A lot of vets get PTSD after seeing action in war. They have these fears that came from the trauma of seeing so many terrible things and fearing for their life. But now the fears don't fit into their daily life. Some even have flashbacks that make it seem like they are right there in the middle of combat again. The same thing can happen to people who've been abused."

"So what do we do?"

"She needs a therapist."

Joshua laughed. "And where will she get the money for that—from her trust fund?"

"What about your dad?"

Joshua's face grew stony.

"What about him?"

"He's bound to have insurance, isn't he? I wonder if it

covers mental health?"

"My dad doesn't believe in shrinks."

"Maybe he will for Brody."

Josh shrugged. "It doesn't matter anyway. No one knows where he is. He hasn't been home since Brody left the house."

"Really?"

Josh sniffed. "Probably off somewhere wasted out of his mind. He's such a loser."

Philip was quiet. After a few seconds he cleared his throat. "I have an idea..."

"It's her mom's birthday, Brody. We just can't ignore that."

"But...shouldn't she be doing something with her dad or something?"

"They're going out to dinner, but...even when her mom was sick they always had a little party. Now her dad has a new girlfriend. Jenny's having trouble with that. They don't talk much these days. She already told me she doesn't want to be alone that night. She's afraid she'll get too depressed. We have to be there for her, Chicken. We're her best friends. Especially since we were there with her when...well, you know, when they buried her mom."

"Oh."

Brody's mind wandered back to the terrible day of the funeral. It seemed inconceivable that anyone could ever completely get over the loss of her mother. She hadn't talked to Jenny much since she had moved. But she still cared for her.

"What did Lara say?"

"She thinks it's a great idea. Her parents said it was fine. I think her brother wants to camp with Josh and me. We could set the two tents up down by the barn. I think it will be a great way to keep Jenny's mind off of her mom. Or at least be there for her if she gets down. What do you say? You in?"

The thought of going that close to her father's house frightened Brody to death. But her friend needed her. And Josh would be there. That would make it okay.

"Sure!"

She smiled a crooked smile and tried to sound excited.

"Great! I'll pick you up Friday around 6:30." He wiggled his eyebrows a couple of times. "I have a surprise for you."

What was that boy up to now?

Brody heard the horn honk around 6:20.

That must be Philip and his mom!

She grabbed her bag and rushed down the stairs of the apartment building.

There, on the street, stood Philip in front of a tiny red car. He spread his arms wide. "Well, what do you think?"

Brody walked over to the vehicle. "Is this yours?" she asked, incredulously.

He held up the keys and dangled them in front of her face. "Mom and I went to pick it up yesterday. Dad gave me a couple hundred bucks on it, and I had some money saved up." He looked a little embarrassed. "It's not much, but it's mine!"

"Well, I think it's as cute as can be! I didn't even know you could drive!"

Philip looked offended. "Of course I can drive. I've had my learner's for a year. I passed the driving part on my sixteenth birthday. Mom's not too crazy about me driving on my own, but it saves her a lot of time running me around and stuff."

He opened the passenger side door with an exaggerated sweeping motion. "Shall we?"

Brody smiled and bowed to him before climbing in. The car's interior was stained and worn, but she loved it! When Philip hopped in beside her and started the engine, she snapped her seat belt on with a little thrill of excitement.

He turned to look at her at the car jerked away from the curb. "Next stop: Jenny's."

At Philip's words, Brody felt a little twinge of disappointment, but she ignored it and it went away.

Jenny was waiting on her porch for them when they pulled up. At the sight of Brody, the girl squealed and ran up to her to give her a big hug as they got out of the car. "I've missed you so much! I was so glad when Philip said you were coming!"

Brody smiled and returned her friend's hug. It was nice to see Jenny smile.

Jenny glanced over her shoulder. Her father emerged from the inside of the house. From the look on his face Brody could tell that he was none too pleased about the events taking place before him. He directed his words to Philip.

"I just talked to Mrs. Spence on the phone and she assured me that you boys and girls would be well-supervised." He turned to Jenny. "Now you behave yourself. It's very nice of the Spences to have this little campout. Don't do anything to show disrespect." He eyed Philip suspiciously. "Do you understand, Jennifer?"

"Yes, Daddy." Jenny's face looked sad.

Brody couldn't help noticing that Jenny hopped into the front passenger side door like she belonged there. Brody opened the back door and slid into the small space there.

They were off. Brody's heart soared as the little car drove miles and miles away from town. She felt free for the first time in a long time. All of the windows were down (no air conditioning) and the wind blew in her face, leaving her breathless and smiling.

She checked off familiar landmarks in her mind as they drew nearer to the land she had always loved. She watched the trees go by, framed in the window like perfect pieces of art. To her surprise, the closer they came to her childhood home, the less fearful she became. Something about the smell of summer coming in the air, the blueness of the sky, the way the leaves moved in the breeze...no matter what had happened to her under these skies they would always be her home. She sighed heavily at the realization that she had missed these old dirt roads.

Philip looked at her apprehensively in the rearview. "You okay?"

Brody smiled. "Perfectly fine."

Philip, still watching her in the mirror, smiled at her tone. "Glad to hear it, Chicken. Glad to hear it."

They pulled into Lara's driveway and Philip pulled the emergency brake up with a clicking noise. "Well, here we are."

Brody could see Josh down by the barn helping Dean set up a tent. One tent was already completely up, zippered door flapping in the breeze. They dropped what they were doing when they saw the other three pull up. Josh came running up the hill.

Philip got out of the car and opened the door for Jenny. "Come on out, Butterfly."

So I'm a chicken and Jenny's a butterfly, Brody thought. *Great.*

"You Dog!" Josh was panting after his quick climb. "Is this really yours?" He was walking around the car, admiring the little red bug.

"You bet! And I'm broke to prove it! My whole life savings down the drain. Good thing I start working this summer."

Seeing the longing on Josh's face, Brody ached for her brother. Even if there ever was enough money for a car in their family, their dad would drink that away too. She looked away from Josh. His face only reminded her of everything that was wrong with their life.

Everyone looked up as the screen door banged shut and Lara walked up the drive.

"Hey, you guys!" Her eyes turned cold as they looked at Brody. "I didn't think you would come."

Very quickly Brody realized her mistake. She hadn't talked to Lara since she left her father's home. What kind of best friend would do something like that? That was the second time this year she had let Lara down. Hadn't Lara told her after their last misunderstanding that friends were supposed to be there for each other, no matter what? Brody felt ashamed. She had been so caught up in her own fears that she hadn't thought of anyone else. Of course Lara was angry with her. The question was: how could she make the other girl understand? And was she ready to open up about what had happened?

Brody didn't have time to ponder these questions; Lara swung around and directed them all to follow with their things down to the campsite.

The girls put their things in the tent that was already up and the boys resumed erecting the other one.

"Come on, you two," Lara gestured to Brody and Jenny. "Mom made pizza. She said we could picnic down here if we carry it down ourselves. I've already put a cooler with drinks over there. All we need is pizza and plates!"

The boys started making grunting noises at the mention of food. Just as they started to cheer and jeer the whole tent fell down on top of them.

"Man," Joshua kidded Dean, "I thought you were in the Boy Scouts! This is one sorry tent job!"

Dean picked up an old dried-out cow patty and hurled it at Josh.

Josh dodged and retaliated. Soon it was a war.

Philip ran up to the house. Breathless, he burst through the kitchen door. "I can't hang with these country boys! Flying cow manure is too much for me!"

The girls looked at each other. "EEEEEooooeeeewwwwwwww!" they said in unison.

Mrs. Spence put her hands on her hips. "Let me handle this." She walked out onto the back porch. "Hey, you two!" she yelled. "Quit that! Quit that right now! Get up here and wash your hands or there'll be no pizza for you!"

She came back in, muttering something about taking the country out of the boy...

The threat of removal of food was all it took. Dean and Josh raced up to the house, flinging a couple last cow bombs as they ran.

After everyone had eaten and they picked up the campsite, the boys went to gather firewood. The girls busied themselves arranging the firestones in a circle. The sun was setting rapidly, and the air was growing crisp and cool. Lara was being civil to Brody, for which she was thankful. But still, she couldn't help remembering the last night she spent here, when her heart had been overjoyed to learn that Lara still wanted to be her best friend. Brody didn't know how to bridge the gap between them. Her heart sank at the thought of losing Lara's friendship. Could Lara forgive her silence a second time?

Brody was deep in thought. She saw Lara reach over and pat Jenny on the shoulder. Her voice was concerned. "How you doin'?"

Jenny's lip quivered a little at Lara's kindness. She drew in her breath. "I'm as good as I can be. Being here with you guys helps. And with Philip." Jenny smiled shyly.

Brody walked over to join the two girls. Lara bristled a little when she drew near.

"You really like him, don't you, Jenny?" Brody asked.

Jenny's smile grew wider and her cheeks flushed. She nodded. "The best thing that ever happened to me was when you invited me to go to church with you guys, Brody. Philip is so...he's so grown up and so...responsible. He has helped me so much since Mom's been gone. I don't know how I could make it without him. He's so-o-o wise. Does that make sense?"

Part of Brody was aching inside and she wasn't sure why. "Yeah, sure...I know what you mean. He always knows just the right thing to say. He's like a—" she swallowed hard—"like a brother to me. He's helped me through some stuff too. And church. He's the one who showed me about church. That has made a difference for me too."

Jenny eyed Brody cautiously. "Why haven't you been coming with us on Sundays then? Philip is really worried about you, you know."

Brody dropped her eyes. "I don't know. Just

everything changing so fast. I just haven't felt like being with anyone or talking to anybody."

Lara snorted at her last statement.

"Lara, I'm sorry I..."

The boys reentering camp interrupted their conversation.

The three of them were carrying a tree that was as long as a house. They were laughing so hard they could barely stand up.

Lara jumped to her feet. "What in the world!"

They dropped the log at the girls' feet and fell on the ground, howling with laughter.

"What on earth is so funny?"

The girls were starting to giggle just watching their friends acting so silly.

Philip was gasping for air. "You should've seen us (gasp) trying to get that tree down (hiccup) hill. It was like (puffpuff) a log-rolling contest gone bad!"

Josh howled. He lowered his voice in a mocking tone to imitate Dean. "Here, let me take care of this. I know these woods like the back of my hand."

They all laughed harder.

Dean chimed in. "We all (puff) thought it was rooted, even though it looked (snicker) dead. So we all three were pulling on it (gasp) and it just started rolling, and we rolled right along with it...all the way down the ravine..." He was laughing so hard he couldn't finish.

The girls were not amused. They took in the filthy appearance of the guys and rolled their eyes in disgust. Lara got up and kicked the log.

"What are we supposed to do with this? We can't put this on a fire! What in the world were you guys thinking?"

Dean laughed even harder. "The bigger the better?" He howled.

Lara frowned at him.

Like a magician performing his grand finale, Dean pulled a small hatchet from a case on his belt. "I vill make short vork of monster log wif dees!" It was a bad German accent. Or was it dork?

The other two boys rolled.

Dean set at the log with gusto. In a matter of minutes he had two gigantic fire logs stacked together inside the stone circle like a teepee. The others gathered twigs and leaves and stuck them around the base to help get the fire started. Before long, they had a roaring fire going. The rest of monster log made an excellent bench to sit on while they watched the fingers of fire rise into the sky.

Philip and Jenny sat close together on the log. Josh and Dean sat on either side of the cozy couple. Lara and

Brody were on the ground below, resting lazily on a sleeping bag. Six pairs of eyes were fixed on the fire.

Brody gave a long sigh of contentment. It was a beautiful night, the stars were out, and she was with some of her favorite people. The crackling of the fire sent electricity though the air and everyone's face glowed with the warmth of friendship. Even Lara seemed to have let go of her grudge against Brody momentarily.

All of a sudden Philip stood up. He glanced at his watch.

"Before midnight there's something we have to do...I almost don't want to because it feels so good just to be here." He looked down at Jenny. "I'll be right back."

He disappeared up the hill. Everyone looked quizzically at Jenny. She shrugged. Brody noticed that her eyes were shining.

Everyone looked expectantly in the direction that Philip had gone. Eventually there came a faint glow slowly approaching. Philip's face was illumined in the night by the candles. When Brody realized what he was doing, she started to cry.

They all began to sing simultaneously. Voices trembling, eyes wet...

"Happy Birthday to you,

Happy Birthday to you,

Happy Birthday, dear Mrs. Burnside...

Happy Birthday to you."

The only sound that could be heard was the crickets when Philip walked over to Jenny with the cake. "Make a wish," he murmured.

Jenny closed her eyes briefly, tears readily streaming. When she opened them she was smiling. *A heartbreaking smile*, thought Brody. Jenny blew out the candles in one soft breath. She looked up at Philip and through her tears mouthed, "thank you," then dabbed her eyes with a napkin.

No one said anything for a while.

Finally Dean broke the silence. "Are we going to eat that cake or what?"

Everyone laughed, and Lara went in the barn to get some more paper plates.

It was getting late. No one really felt like telling ghost stories. Dean and Josh decided to call it a night, citing their log-rolling incident as too much excitement for the day. Josh squeezed Brody's shoulder on the way into the boys' tent.

Brody felt a momentary panic at his departure from

the group.

Don't be silly, she told herself. *You'll be fine. He's only a few steps away.*

The remaining four sat in comfortable silence for a time. It was Lara who broke the quiet.

"So, Brody." Her voice was cool. "Why did you disappear this time? I mean, you didn't even call to say good-bye. I had to find out from Jenny, who found out from Philip, who found out from Josh that you had changed schools. I thought that should have been something a best friend should have known about. So I guess that means..."

Philip was trying to signal Lara to stop. Brody looked at her shoes and prayed for the right words. She prayed that the Lord would help her share this so that her friendship with Lara might be mended; and so that whatever it was in her heart that was broken might be healed.

"It's OK, Philip. I'm OK. I should have told you all. I'm just not good at this...I'm not good at talking. I'm sorry, Lara. You have been the best friend anyone could ask for. I don't blame you for being mad. And I would understand if you can't forgive me. You see, when I left, I wasn't thinking about anyone else but myself. And I've had a hard time ever since...a hard time just getting up and going about life."

Brody swallowed hard and took a deep breath.

"Something bad happened. My dad, well, you all know how he drinks. And since Mom left, it's only gotten worse. Josh and I never saw him. He was gone to work when we got up for school, or else he never came home the night before. The only times we saw him he was drunk or passed out. But we were okay, just a little worried about him.

"Then this one night, I heard him come home. Only it wasn't just him. This—" she wiped her eyes and tried not to see the man's face—"this man brought him home because he was so bad off. I tried to hide, but he saw me..."

Brody's whole body started to shake as she relived that night. "He came after me...and hit me. If it wasn't for Joshua..."

Joshua, who must have been listening from inside the tent, came out and put his arms around his sister. Brody was crying quietly, unable to stop the images from looming before her in her mind.

"Shhh...it's okay, Bro. You don't have to say any more. It's okay. Shhh." Josh stroked her hair and comforted her.

Lara moved over and put her arms around Brody too. Soon Philip and Jenny did the same.

When Brody woke up the next morning she was surrounded by the arms of all her friends, huddled together on the tiny sleeping bag, under the open sky.

She was glad to spend a little time alone with Philip before the others woke up. Even though she was happy for him and Jenny, Philip would always be special to her. They were quietly tidying up the campsite, trying to figure out what to do with the monster log.

"You know," she said shyly, "what you did for Jenny last night was unbelievable. It was very sweet and I know it made missing her mom a little better."

Philip smiled a little sheepishly. "I just wish I could take away all the pain she has from missing her mom. But...I know only God can help her with that."

"I don't know. You're doing a pretty good job," she kidded him.

He smiled. "We're taking it slow. We're too young really to date. Mom is concerned. And you saw her dad. It will really take some work to win his trust."

They laughed.

"Yeah, you might be right about that," Brody said.

Philip's face got serious. "But, Bro, what about you? Why couldn't you tell us how much you were hurting? It kills me that you went through all that alone. When Josh told me what happened, I knew you needed us more than ever. I didn't want to scare you, but I had to do something."

"So, was this whole thing a plan of yours?"

Brody tried to sound stern, but she was touched by his concern.

Philip looked sheepish.

"Forgive me? I wouldn't have had to be so sneaky if you'd only trusted us. Why didn't you tell us from the start, Bro?"

"I don't know. I was ashamed. Ashamed and afraid. I still feel afraid most of the time. It was so scary, Philip."

"Please promise me you will never keep anything like that from me again. I wasn't kidding when I said you were like my sister. And, Bro?"

"Hmmm?"

"You have to come back to church. Don't you remember what God said to Abraham? 'Do not be afraid. I am your shield, your very great reward.' "

She had forgotten the promise. As she contemplated this, Philip kept right on talking. "The Bible says during times of trouble we should take refuge in the shelter of His wings..."

The king is enthralled by your beauty; honor Him, for He is your Lord...

Clothed with splendor, wrapped in light...

Great is His love, higher than the heavens;

His faithfulness reaches to the skies...

Take refuge in the shelter of His wings,

Find comfort in His love...

Brody jerked up her head. She heard the song as clearly as she had heard it that day in the roses. "What did you say?"

"I said you have to come back to church..."

"No, no, not that...after that, what did you say?"

"What? The Bible says we should take refuge in the shelter of His..."

"Where?"

"What?"

"Where in the Bible does it say that?"

Philip shrugged. "In Psalms, I think. I think it's in chapter sixty-one or sixty-two, why?"

"I knew it! Philip, I need to get a new Bible!"

"What are you talking about, Brody?"

Brody sighed happily. She felt like she had just found a huge piece of herself. "Nothing. Nothing. Can you do me a favor?"

"Yeah, sure, anything."

"Will you swing me by Dad's on the way out this morning? There is something there that I need to get."

With the bird tucked safely in her pocket, Brody almost felt like her old self again. She smiled at Philip's Mom as she slid into the back seat of the station wagon.

"Hello, Mrs. Pauley."

"Hello, Brody. It's nice to see you again. Will you be able to come to dinner after church?"

"I'd love to."

Mrs. Pauley smiled in the rearview. "And we'd love it if you would. We've missed you."

Brody stepped out into the sunlight. If felt so good. She had told her story twice now, and she had survived. She even felt better for it. It was a little easier to say out loud this time.

Philip had made an appointment with the pastor for her after church. At first, Brody wasn't sure about it, but when she rubbed the bird in her pocket she knew that it was what she was supposed to do. The bird had somehow given her the courage to get through the last hour, revealing her secrets to a stranger.

But she had liked his eyes. Pastor Blake was a kindly man. He was going to try to arrange for her to see a therapist through the church. He thought that she needed more help than he could give. Just the thought of trying to put this behind her gave Brody a huge sense of relief. For the first time in her life she did not feel like she had to handle everything on her own. It felt so good to depend on others, to depend on God. She trusted Him—that He would take her where she needed to be for healing.

She searched the parking lot for Philip's little red car. He said he would be back to take her home. There he was! But who was that he was talking to? There were two men leaning into Philip's car, deep in conversation. The sun was right in her eyes so she couldn't quite make them out.

As she drew near, Philip raised his hand in greeting. The tallest man stood up straight, looking extremely uncomfortable. He was wearing a suit and a tie and Brody almost didn't recognize him.

Daddy!

She froze in her steps. She didn't know whether to run to him or away from him. She felt a surge of joy at the sight of him...they hadn't seen him for a couple months. No one knew where he was. In the back of her mind had been a fear that he was gone forever. She wondered if he was disappointed in her. Maybe he blamed her for what had happened. But she was surprised at the joy in her heart.

I guess I do love him after all, she mused.

But hand in hand with her joy was the same old fear. What was he up to now? Was he drunk and going to make a scene? What had he said to Philip? Why was he here?

History gave many reasons to be suspicious of her

father. But in the end her love won out. She walked cautiously toward the three figures that were all standing at attention for her.

"You clean up real nice," she nudged Josh, who was wearing khaki pants and a tie. He smiled weakly.

Brody turned her eyes to her father. He was looking at his shoes, holding a hat in his hands.

"Daddy?"

When he looked up there was hope in his eyes...and shame...and fear.

"We've been waiting for you for nearly an hour. Josh and I decided we wanted to come to the church service today. But we were a little late so we had to sit in the back. That was just fine with me because it gave me a chance to see my little girl without worrying she would run away..." He looked down at his shoes again. "I told myself I would never look you in the eyes again until I was clean and sober."

He looked up and met Brody's eyes boldly. "I stand before you a changed man. I know I've not been much of a father to you and your brothers and sister, and maybe it's a little late, but I want a second chance. Brody, I never want to hurt you again. I'm so sorry about everything..." His voice broke down a little but he regained his composure.

"Would you mind terribly if I started coming to church with you on Sundays? My mama was a great woman of

God. You may not believe this, but when I was a young'un I sang in the children's choir. I went to Sunday school every week."

Grandma Pat's image flashed before Brody's eyes. What would that gentlewoman say about her son's sudden change of character? Brody knew her grandmother would be overjoyed.

"I'd like that, Daddy," she said in a soft voice.

As if he'd been holding his breath, a loud burst of air escaped through J.D.'s lips. His shoulders relaxed and he lunged toward his daughter. Before Brody knew what was happening he had caught her up in his arms and was squeezing the daylights out of her. She saw Josh smiling over their father's shoulders.

Forgiveness, she thought. *What a beautiful thing.*

Epilogue

Brody wasn't sure why she had brought the little bird to school with her.

It was the dream, the night before. The tiny creature was alive, gloriously so! Brody had felt such joy when she watched the stony wings turn to feather and fly! The creature had landed in her hands. She had kissed the feathery head, then set the bird free.

Her heart was filled with gratitude as she watched the rainbow of colors soar away from her in that dream. But what did it mean?

She rubbed the smooth stone in her pocket and heard that familiar chirruping voice in her head.

He is near.

Brody looked around. The great hall was silent. A huge enclosed glass patio flanked the school's entryway. She looked beyond the open double doors to the patio beyond. No one. She shrugged and began walking quickly to her homeroom.

But as she walked away a tugging in her heart made her turn and look back. As she did so, she heard a peal of thunder and a torrential rain began to fall. In the distance, just feet from the shelter of the patio, a tall figure dressed all in black emerged. He was soaked all the way down to his skin. Brody was paralyzed as she watched him. Sensing her eyes on him, he inclined his face to her and their eyes met.

Yes. It is him.

To her amazement, Brody began to walk toward the dark figure. He too began to move toward her. When they met in the shelter of the patio, Klaio was in her hand. One last rub with her thumb and she lovingly slipped the bird into his calloused palm.

"Take good care of her," she whispered. "Keep her close to your heart."

Then Brody turned and walked away, leaving the young man puzzling over his unexpected gift.

I shall miss her, Lord.

She will always be a part of you, Beloved.

Klaio thought of the many hearts with whom she had been one throughout the years.

Yes, my Lord, she will.

Want to Know More?
Great questions to think about and discuss

1. What are some of Brody's feelings as she goes through her parents' divorce? Why do you think she felt that way?

Have you ever gone through a time when you felt alone? When you wondered if there really is a God? And if there is, if He cares about you and what's going on in your life? Tell the story.

2. Read the story of Abraham's call in Genesis 12:1-9. Now read Hebrews 11:8-10. What did it take for Abraham to obey God when He asked him to leave his home?

Do you think you would have reacted the way Abraham did? Why or why not?

3. Read Genesis 15:5-6. What do these verses mean to you? Why do you think these verses meant a lot to Brody?

Is there a Bible verse that you treasure? If so, write it down and carry it with you as encouragement. If not, think about your life and the things you love...what's most important to you. Ask those who know the Bible well or use a Bible concordance to find verses that address those topics.

4. When Brody finds out her mother is pregnant, how does she react? How does Philip react? Who do you think was right? Explain your answer.

Then read Matthew 7:1-5. What do these verses mean to you?

5. Have you wrongly judged someone? If so, who (if you can't say it aloud, write about it in your journal)? Is there any way in which you can make the situation right? What will you choose to do differently next time?

Now read Hebrews 2:8-13. What kind of quality should we show in judging others? Do you see that quality in yourself? Why or why not? How could you become more sensitive to others?

5. After Brody is attacked, she withdraws from God and from her friends and family. Why do you think she did this? Have you ever been so hurt that you didn't want to be around anyone...and you found it hard to trust others? Tell the story to a trusted friend, or write about it in your journal.

Read Joshua 1:9. Was Brody really alone during her difficult time? Why or why not? The next time you're feeling lonely and hurting, how can reading the words of Joshua 1:9 give you a different kind of perspective?

6. What do you think happens next in Brody's story? Make up another chapter to the book and share it with your friends. **I'd love to see it too. Email it to me at laraj@suddenlink.net.**

About the Author

LAURA J. BOGGESS loves to read. She has channeled her love of words into writing since she was a young girl. As a child growing up in impoverished Appalachia, her family faced the all-too-common problems of parental alcoholism and divorce. Her experiences led to the desire to help others heal through story. Laura believes that if you can capture a child's imagination, he or she is capable of overcoming anything.

Laura obtained her master's degree in Clinical Psychology in 1992. She currently works in a medical rehabilitation facility where she counsels patients with acquired brain injury and their families. She has also worked as a Director of Children's Ministries and is active in the women's ministry at her church.

Laura lives in Hurricane, West Virginia, with her husband, Jeff, their two boys, Teddy and Jeffrey, and their Boston terrier, Lucy Mae. She has been published in *the Charleston Gazette*, *Pray!* magazine, *Proverbs 31 Women* magazine, and Crosswalk.com.

For further information about Laura J. Boggess:
http://Lauraboggess.homestead.com
www.oaktara.com

Printed in the United States
206095BV00001B/280/P